Little Miss, BIG SIS

written by Amy Krouse Rosenthal · illustrated by Peter H. Reynolds

HARPER

An Imprint of HarperCollinsPublishers

The big news is this:

Little Miss

will be a big sis.

Will be a big sis?

WILL BE A BIG SIS!

Waiting and waiting.

Anticipating.

Then...   Ow.

NOW!

WOW!

What now?

Sleep.   Fuss.   Eat.

Repeat.

Cry. Cry.

(Lullaby?)

Do not despair—I'll help care!

From there, EVERYWHERE...

Stay near crib.

Help with bib.

(What a sib!)

Baby grows.
Smile shows.

Such cute toes.

Hugging, holding.
Love unfolding.

Singing. Swinging.

Real fun beginning.

Crawling, crawling.
Falling, falling.

Lap, clap.

(Need a nap!)

Funny faces.
Warm embraces.
Giggly chases.

No! Not the vases!

Sure, sometimes takes toys.

And sometimes annoys.

But always supports.

You make the
bestest forts!

Admired.

Inspired.

Forever protected.

Forever connected.

And just as suspected...
from that first hug and kiss...

the most wonderful
BIG SIS!

To Beth, Joe, and Kate
for letting me be their big sis
—A.K.R.

To Henry Rocket Reynolds and his big sis, Sarah,
and Renie Reynolds and her big sis, Jane
—P.H.R.

Library of Congress Cataloging-in-Publication Data

Rosenthal, Amy Krouse.
  Little Miss, big sis / by Amy Krouse Rosenthal ; illustrated by Peter H. Reynolds. — First edition.
    pages cm
  Summary: Illustrations and simple, rhyming text follow Little Miss as she learns to be a wonderful big sister.
  ISBN 978-0-06-230203-8 (hardcover)
  [1. Stories in rhyme. 2. Sisters—Fiction. 3. Babies—Fiction.] I. Reynolds, Peter, illustrator. II. Title.
PZ8.3.R7285Lit 2015   2014005878
[E]—dc23   CIP
                                                                                                          AC

Typography by Peter H. Reynolds 15 16 17 18 19   SCP   10 9 8 7 6 5 4 3 2 1 ❖ First Edition